Operation BANANA

Tony Bradman

Illustrated by
Tania Rex

Barrington  Stoke

First published in 2023 in Great Britain by
Barrington Stoke Ltd
18 Walker Street, Edinburgh, EH3 7LP

www.barringtonstoke.co.uk

Text © 2023 Tony Bradman
Illustrations © 2023 Tania Rex

A CIP catalogue record for this book is available
from the British Library upon request

ISBN: 978-1-80090-187-2

Printed by Hussar Books, Poland

Operation
BANANA

For my mum and dad, children of the war

CONTENTS

CONTENTS

Chapter 1

Doom and Gloom

North London, November 1942

It all started the night Susan's mum burst into tears at dinner.

Susan and Mum were sitting at the kitchen table in their flat with the radio on. It was the BBC News at Six O'Clock, but Susan wasn't listening. She was too excited about what was on her plate.

As a special treat, the butcher had let Mum have two pork chops. They were tiny and a bit tough. But Susan couldn't remember the last time they'd had meat for dinner, and she really wanted to enjoy it.

Mum was still wearing her khaki work overalls and had a red scarf tied up over her fair hair. Susan's hair was brown and cut in a neat bob, and she was wearing her school uniform: an old navy-blue pinafore dress and a white blouse.

Suddenly, Mum began to cry, the tears running down her cheeks and dripping onto the table. Susan sat there for a moment with a piece of pork on her fork, halfway to her mouth. Then she jumped up and hugged Mum.

"I'm sorry, love," Mum said softly. "I just can't bear it any more."

"The chops *are* a bit hard to chew," said Susan. "But they're not that bad."

"I don't mean the chops," said Mum. "Although I do wish we could have something nice to eat for once. It's just that this blasted war has been going on so long I've forgotten what it's like to be happy. Listen to the news – it's all doom and gloom ..."

Mum pointed at the radio and started to sob again. Susan hugged her more tightly and began to listen to what the reporter was saying.

Mum was right. The news was a list of terrible things – mostly defeats for Britain and its allies. German submarines had sunk more British ships in the North Atlantic. German soldiers were about to capture yet another city in Russia – a place called Stalingrad. And German planes had attacked the city of Canterbury in Kent. They had dropped lots of bombs and killed thirty people.

"I see what you mean, Mum," said Susan. "Tell you what – go and relax in the front room while I do the washing-up. Then I'll make you a nice cup of tea."

"Thanks, love. I really don't know what I'd do without you," said Mum. She blew her nose. "I'm just tired. It's been really tough at the factory this week ..."

Susan put their plates in the sink. She had been helping Mum almost as long as she could remember. They'd had to look after each other since the war had begun in 1939.

Dad had joined the Army right away, and he'd been sent off to fight in North Africa. He wrote long funny letters full of jokes and drawings of camels, but it wasn't the same as having him at home. And of course they worried about him all the time.

In fact, they hadn't had a letter from him for a few months, and that was odd. There had been loads of fighting in North Africa over the summer, especially at a place called El Alamein. That name came up a lot.

Now Susan thought about it, she worked out they had been at war with horrible old Hitler and his nasty Nazis for over three years. Three years of bombs and being scared and never having enough to eat. Three years of bad news that only got worse.

The Germans kept winning. They hadn't invaded Britain yet, thank goodness, but nobody knew when the war might end – or who would win.

Susan filled the kettle and put it on the gas ring. It had been Mum who had got them through it so far, she thought. Mum had kept her going through the Blitz, when the Germans had bombed London night after night.

Just like thousands of people all over London, as soon as they heard the warning sirens, Susan and Mum had to rush to take shelter in a Tube station. The nearest Tube station to their flats was at Finsbury Park. It was only a couple of streets away.

Sometimes, as they sat with all the others in the Tube station, they could hear the bombs going off in the streets above. Susan

remembered the cheery song that Mum had always sung to keep her calm when the bombs were falling: "Pack up your troubles in your old kitbag and smile, smile, smile ..."

Suddenly, Susan felt bad – she hadn't been looking after Mum well enough. Mum hadn't smiled for ages, and Susan wished she'd noticed before. Why hadn't she done something sooner to help Mum?

A few moments later, Susan went into the front room with the tea things on a tray – a teapot, their best china cups and saucers, a nice little jug for the milk.

"Here you are, Madam," Susan said in a posh voice. "Tea is served ..."

Mum didn't answer. She was curled up on the settee, asleep. Her eyes were shut tight, and she twitched a couple of times as if she were having a bad dream.

And that's when Susan decided she really
had to cheer Mum up.

The only question was – how?

Chapter 2

The Black Market

The next morning, Susan and her mum got up and had their normal breakfast – toast with a scrape of marge and Marmite, and big mugs of tea. Then they put on their coats and went out.

Mum's bus stop was not far from their block of flats. Her job was very important. The factory where she worked made radio parts for Spitfires – the RAF fighter planes that defended Britain against the German air force, the Luftwaffe.

Susan's school was just across the local park, a ten-minute walk. They always went as far as the main road together, then said goodbye on the corner.

"See you later, love," said Mum, kissing her. "And don't worry, I'm fine."

"If I believed that, I'd believe anything," Susan muttered to herself as Mum walked away, heading for the bus stop. "I might only be eleven, but I'm not daft."

She turned into the street that led to her school. It was a cold day, the sky was grey and there would probably be rain later. The street was busy – people hurrying to work, buses and trams going past.

Most days, Susan didn't take much notice of what went on around her – Mum often said Susan lived in a world of her own. But today she couldn't help looking at everything and everyone that she passed.

She saw that things were grim. There was a lot of bomb damage in the streets and plenty of empty spaces where whole buildings had been destroyed. People looked tired and worried, their clothes old, their shoes scuffed. Susan had a feeling the rest of the country was the same.

She came to her school at last and walked through the gates. At least good old Malcolm Road Juniors hadn't been bombed, she thought. It was a bit shabby, but it had been built ages ago, in the time of Queen Victoria, so of course it was getting old and worn out.

Some kids were in the playground, a few boys kicking a football around, a group of girls skipping with a long rope and singing a rhyme as they jumped.

"All right, Susan?" said a voice behind her. It was Jimmy Ryan. Jimmy was short, and scruffy in his baggy shorts and grey jacket. His hair always stood on end like he'd just had an electric shock.

Jimmy and Susan had been best mates since the school was evacuated in 1939 to a village in the Sussex countryside. They'd been put together in the same billet – a farm run by an old couple who weren't very nice to them.

Children all over the country had been evacuated because the government thought the Germans would start bombing cities as soon as the war began. But that didn't happen, so most kids came home pretty soon.

The bombing started the year after that. But when the Blitz began in the autumn of 1940, Mum said she wasn't going to send Susan away again – she'd missed her too much the first time. That was fine with Susan. She had felt just the same.

"Actually, I'm *not* all right," Susan told Jimmy as they sat down on a bench. "I'm worried about my mum."

"Why, what's up with her?" Jimmy asked. "Is she sick?"

"No, she isn't," said Susan. "She's definitely not very happy though."

"I think a lot of grown-ups feel the same way," Jimmy said. "My mum is always moaning about the war. You should hear her go on about rationing."

"Rationing is awful," said Susan. "Nobody likes going without all the things they need, do they?"

Rationing meant you were only allowed to have a small amount of normal everyday things, even food.

When you bought something, you had to show shopkeepers your ration book, and you had to hand over the right coupons so as to be able to buy anything at all. The Germans were sinking lots of ships that were bringing food and other important supplies to Britain.

"Well, *there's* someone who doesn't have to go without," said Jimmy.

He was looking at a girl who had just come through the school gates. Her long red hair was in two pigtails, and she was wearing a fancy new coat and a pair of shiny shoes.

The girl's name was Doreen, and everyone knew her dad was a real crook. He wasn't in the Army, the Navy or the RAF – he was in the black market. He bought and sold all sorts of stuff that had been stolen, and he made lots of money out of it.

"I'll bet she gets plenty of nice things to eat too," Susan muttered as Doreen walked past them with her nose in the air.

Just then Susan had an idea. "Hang on," she said. "I know what to do now. Mum said she'd like to eat something nice for once ..."

"That would definitely cheer *me* up," said Jimmy. "I dream about food all the time – sausages, ice cream, sweets. I'd give anything for a bar of chocolate."

"Me too, but that's all a bit obvious. It has to be really special for Mum, something that will surprise her. No, even better ... something that will make her smile."

Jimmy looked at Susan for a second,
thinking hard. Then he grinned.

"How about a banana?" he said. "Or maybe
a whole bunch?"

"Now you're talking!" said Susan, grinning
back at him.

A banana would be perfect.

Chapter 3

A Hard Task

Just then their headmaster, Mr Jenner, came out of the school building and rang the bell for the children to line up. They had Assembly in the hall, with prayers and hymns, then went to their classrooms.

Susan and Jimmy were in Mrs Robinson's class. She had retired before the war started but came back because most of the younger teachers had been called up into the Forces.

They started with Arithmetic, which Susan usually liked – she was good at sums. Today, however, she couldn't concentrate. All she could think about was … bananas.

You could still get apples and pears in the shops, or at the street markets. But Susan couldn't remember when she had last seen a banana, let alone actually *eaten* one.

That was why it would be such a great surprise for Mum. But the more Susan thought about it, the more she knew that finding a banana was going to be tricky.

"I wouldn't even know where to start," said Jimmy at playtime. They were standing at the side of the playground, watching the others playing football or skipping. "There might be an easy way," he went on. "Why don't you just ask Doreen to talk to her dad? I'll bet he can get you as many bunches of bananas as you want."

"Oh no, I can't do that!" said Susan. "My mum and dad would be so cross if they found out. Before he went away, my dad made me promise to be good."

That was one thing Susan *did* remember. In her mind she could still see Dad, standing by the front door in his uniform, ready to leave, kitbag packed. He had given her a lovely silver locket and chain that had belonged to his granny. He

said that it would help Susan to remember him
while he was away.

"Take care of your mum for me, sweetheart,"
he'd said. "And be a good girl."

She pulled the locket out from under her
blouse to look at it. Suddenly, she felt someone
staring at her – it was Doreen. Susan tucked
the locket back under her blouse. Doreen gave
a shrug and walked away.

"Well, if you don't want to ask Doreen's dad," Jimmy was saying, "then I reckon you'll need to do some thinking."

Jimmy was right, of course. When they went back into their classroom, Susan got out her exercise book and turned to an empty page at the back.

She thought for a moment, chewing the end of her pencil. Then she wrote OPERATION BANANA in capital letters right across the top of the page and drew two lines with her ruler

underneath. After all, the Army called their plans "Operations", didn't they?

She wrote down the first part of her plan:
1. *Find banana to cheer up Mum*. But that was as far as she got. No matter how hard she tried, she couldn't think of anything else, so she sat there, chewing her pencil again. Maybe she needed some more help ...

"You should ask Mr Jenner," said Jimmy later at lunchtime. All the children were eating their school dinners in the hall – tiny spam fritters followed by tiny slices of jam roly-poly. "I mean, he *is* a headmaster, so he probably knows everything."

"Good idea!" said Susan, and went to see Mr Jenner. He didn't have a secretary any more. The last one had gone off and joined the Wrens, the Women's Royal Navy. Susan walked past her empty desk and knocked on Mr Jenner's door.

"Come!" he called out, and she went inside. His room had lots of bookshelves and cupboards, and a window that looked out onto the playground.

Mr Jenner sat behind his big desk. He had white hair and he looked tired and old. Just like Mrs Robinson, he had retired before the war but had come back to help. Susan quickly told him why she had come to see him.

"It's a lovely idea, Susan, and I'm sure your mum would be pleased," he said. "But you've set yourself a hard task. Before the war, we got bananas from places like Jamaica and Barbados in the West Indies, and from West Africa too. But all the ships that used to bring bananas are now full of soldiers coming here to help us fight the Nazis. They might have a bit of room for some cargo, but not much."

"So you don't think I'll find any?" Susan said softly.

"Ah, now I didn't say that, Susan. You're a bright girl, and I bet you can do most things you set your mind to. I don't think you'll find any bananas in the shops round here. But there *might* be some at Covent Garden Market, the big fruit and vegetable market in London. You can find all sorts of things there ..."

That afternoon, Mrs Robinson said the class could do some silent reading. That was fine with Susan. She got her reading book out of her desk, but she spent more time thinking about what Mr Jenner had said. She knew exactly what to do now.

She turned to the Operation Banana page at the back of her exercise book and carefully wrote: *2. Skip school and go to Covent Garden Market ...*

Chapter 4

Skipping School

Mum wasn't so sad at dinner that evening. She didn't do any smiling as they ate the vegetable stew she'd made, but she did talk a bit. Then they listened to the BBC News on the radio again, and Mum's mood darkened.

"There are reports of heavy fighting at El Alamein," the voice on the radio said. "The Germans have made several new attacks, and our Army is fighting back ..."

"Oh no," Mum groaned, and her eyes filled up with tears all over again. "Your dad might well be right in the middle of all that. I just hope nothing happens to him!"

Susan felt the same. She really wished one of Dad's funny letters would arrive, but at least now she had her plan to cheer Mum up.

*

The next morning, Susan set off with Mum as normal. But after Mum went to catch her bus, Susan didn't go on to school. Instead, she waited for Jimmy on the corner of Malcolm Road. He'd said he would take the morning off too and go with her to Covent Garden Market.

"I feel bad about skipping school," said Susan as they walked to the bus stop. They were going to catch a bus from there to the West End of London. "My dad wouldn't like it."

"It's all in a good cause," said Jimmy. "Besides, I bet Mrs Robinson won't notice. There are a lot of kids in our class, and she can hardly keep track of us."

Susan hoped he was right and tried to stop worrying about it. She knew what bus to catch. Mum had often taken her down to the West End to see the sights and do some window shopping. Susan felt quite excited once they were on the bus.

"Fares, please!" the conductor called out. Susan paid for her ticket and Jimmy's as well.

Mum gave her pocket money sometimes, and Susan had saved as much as she could. She had emptied her piggy bank that morning and counted the money. She had a grand total of three shillings and fourpence halfpenny. She had no idea how much bananas cost. She crossed the fingers of both hands and hoped she'd have enough.

Susan and Jimmy got off the bus at Piccadilly Circus. They stood there for a moment, just looking around. The statue in the middle was covered up with posters that had advice from the government on them – they said things like *Careless Words Cost Lives* and *Buy War Bonds* and *Keep On Smiling!* There were advertising signs on the buildings, and streams of buses and taxis going past.

There were so many people too, most of them wearing uniforms. Susan saw British soldiers, sailors and airmen. She knew London was also full of people from the countries Hitler

and the Nazis had conquered – France, Holland and Belgium, Denmark and Norway, Poland and Greece.

She saw men and women in lots of different uniforms. There were soldiers in London from all over the world – Australia, New Zealand, Canada, the West Indies, Senegal and India, even America.

Susan knew America had been attacked by Japan, who were on Hitler's side, and then America had joined the war to help Britain and its allies.

American soldiers had come across the Atlantic to fight. People called them "Yanks". They talked like the stars in Hollywood movies, and they often gave kids American chewing gum and bars of chocolate. So it was no wonder the Yanks were very popular.

"Let's go and talk to those Yanks," said Jimmy. He was pointing at a big group of American soldiers. "They might have something for us ..."

"Sorry, Jimmy, but we don't have time," said Susan. "Come on, this way."

Covent Garden Market wasn't far from Piccadilly Circus. It was in a building that had a high roof and pillars along the sides. The

streets around it were packed with lorries and carts pulled by horses, and there were lots of people coming to buy and sell.

Everyone was shouting; men called porters carried tottering towers of baskets filled with fruit and vegetables on their heads.

"Well, I've seen lots of fruit and vegetables," said Jimmy after they'd walked around for a

while. "And that's made me feel even more hungry. But I haven't seen any bananas."

"Me neither," said Susan. "But I'm not going to give up yet. Let's ask someone."

Most of the people were too busy to talk. But they found one man at last. He had sold most of his produce and was sitting down, having a nice cup of tea.

"Bananas?" he said, looking as if he wasn't sure what the word meant. "No, we never get any. Some ships bring in a few, but they're snapped up at the docks long before traders like us even see them. Mind you, if you know the right people ..."

He grinned and gave them a big wink, then went back to drinking his tea.

"Er ... thanks," said Susan, then turned away. She walked out, back into the crowded, noisy

street. Jimmy hurried behind her, but it was hard for him to keep up.

"Hang on, Susan!" he said. "Wait for me! What are you going to do now?"

"There's only one thing I can do, isn't there?" she muttered.

She would have to talk to Doreen.

Chapter 5

The Big Surprise

They got back to school at lunchtime and slipped into class with everyone else when playtime was over. Jimmy was right – Mrs Robinson didn't say anything, thank goodness.

They did more Arithmetic, then Mrs Robinson read a chapter from their story book, but Susan wasn't listening. She brooded instead, wishing things were different. But they weren't, and she just had to get on with it.

At the end of the day, she grabbed her coat from the cloakroom and ran after Doreen into the playground. Jimmy came along as well, of course.

"Doreen, could I have a word with you?" said Susan. "Please?"

"Why?" said Doreen, turning to face her. "What do you want?"

"Er ... I was hoping I could ask you for a favour." Susan could feel herself starting to blush. Doreen looked hard at her, but she didn't say anything. She waited for Susan to speak.

"My mum needs cheering up," Susan began, "and I thought if I could get her a ... some ..."

"Oh, for heaven's sake, Susan, spit it out!" said Jimmy. "Sorry, Doreen, she wants you to ask your dad to get her a banana so she can give it to her mum ..."

Jimmy said a bit more about Susan and her mum and bananas, then Susan joined in at last.

Between them, they explained exactly what Susan wanted.

"A banana? Really?" said Doreen, looking puzzled. Then she gave a shrug. "I always knew you two were weird, but my dad says it takes all sorts to make a world."

"So can your dad help or not?" said Susan. "I've got the money to pay."

She took her purse out of her pocket and opened it to show Doreen the coins inside. Doreen peered at them, then looked up at Susan again and grinned.

"Well, it's a start," she said. "But I'll want that locket of yours as well."

"My locket?" said Susan with a small gasp. She was just about to say "No!", then she thought of her mum and how sad she was feeling and did what she had to.

She quickly took off her locket and dropped it into Doreen's hand.

"It might take a few days," said Doreen. "I'll let you know ..."

In fact, it took three days, but Doreen's dad did come good. Doreen handed over a small brown paper bag to Susan in the playground. Jimmy was with her too.

"I hope she enjoys it," said Doreen over her shoulder as she walked off. "Tell her not to eat it all at once. My dad said they're worth more than gold these days."

"Blimey, I can't believe you did it," said Jimmy. "Let's have a look then."

Susan opened the bag, and they stared at the object inside. It was smaller than she had imagined, and not very yellow, either. The skin was quite black and spotty, and one whole end looked dark, almost as if there was something wrong with it.

"Er ... I'm sure it's going to taste absolutely amazing ..." said Jimmy.

42

"Of course it will!" said Susan. But she knew he didn't really think so, and now she began to worry. What if it tasted awful? What if Mum didn't enjoy it?

*

Susan ran home at the end of the day, telling herself she had done the right thing and that everything would be fine. She wanted to get to the flat before Mum got back so she could prepare the big surprise for her. It was all going to be so special ...

In the end, it didn't work out quite the way she had planned. When Mum came in, Susan was standing by the table. She had set out the best tea things and put the banana on a nice plate. Mum stopped and looked at it and then at Susan.

"I got you a banana!" said Susan – and now it was her turn to burst into tears.

Mum rushed over to hug her and ask what was wrong, and soon Mum was crying too, the tears streaming down both of their faces. In the end, Susan told Mum the whole story of Operation Banana – the special mission she had planned to cheer her up.

"Oh, Susan, what a wonderful daughter you are!" Mum said with a big smile. "See, you *have* made me smile again! But I'll be having a word

with that Doreen's dad, you wait and see. Your locket is worth more than a bit of fruit ..."

They saved the banana for after they had eaten dinner. Mum said that they had to share it. She took the skin off and cut it in half, and they ate it with some condensed milk from a

tin. It was a bit mushy but quite sweet, and
Susan didn't like it that much. But she was very
pleased to see that Mum really enjoyed it.

Mum put the radio on, and Susan saw how
her smile vanished when the Six O'Clock News
began. But it soon came back – the news was
good for once.

"Our Army has defeated the Germans
at El Alamein," said the reporter. "It's a
very heavy blow for Hitler and could be an
important turning point in the war."

"You know, I'm beginning to think things aren't too bad after all," said Mum. "There's only one more thing we need now to make us both a lot happier ..."

And two days later, that thing happened. A letter from Dad came at last, a really long one, full of jokes and funny pictures and news of what he had been doing.

Susan read it over and over again. She longed for the day when this terrible war would be over at last. She wanted her dad to walk back through the door, safe and sound.

Somehow she felt sure that day would come.

Historical Note

The Second World War went on for a very long time. It began in September 1939 and went on till 1945. The Allies defeated Nazi Germany at last in May of that year, but the war against Japan went on until September. That's almost six years in total.

So by November 1942, after three years of war, the people of Britain had lived through a lot. The history books say that before 1942, Britain didn't win any battles, and after it we hardly lost any. The turning points were the defeat of the Germans in North Africa and the huge battle of Stalingrad in Russia. The Germans lost an enormous number of

Historical Note

The Second World War went on for a very long time. It began in September 1939 and went on till 1945. The Allies defeated Nazi Germany at last in May of that year, but the war against Japan went on until September. That's almost six years in total.

So by November 1942, after three years of war, the people of Britain had lived through a lot. The history books say that before 1942, Britain didn't win any battles, and after it we hardly lost any. The turning points were the defeat of the Germans in North Africa and the huge battle of Stalingrad in Russia. The Germans lost an enormous number of soldiers there and would never be as strong or dangerous again.

But there was still a long way to go and, as Susan says in the story, nobody knew when the war would end. Everyone was worn out, and most people were very fed up in one way or another. Of course it was tough on the soldiers, sailors and airmen who were fighting. But it was also hard on the people at home, especially mums with young families. They often had to work hard and take care of their children as well.

In fact, there were millions of people like Susan and her mum, and they were just as important in winning the war. That's why I wanted to write their story.

Old and New Money

These days money is very simple – there are one hundred pennies in a pound. But at the time of the Second World War, we still used the old way of dividing money up. There were:

12 pennies in a shilling

20 shillings in a pound

(So there were 240 pennies in a pound!)

There were also more coins – halfpennies, threepenny bits, sixpences, two-shilling pieces and half crowns (two shillings and sixpence!). There was also a small coin called a farthing – a quarter of a penny.

So when Susan emptied her piggy bank, she had "three shillings and fourpence halfpenny".

It wasn't until 1971 that we changed to the way things are now.